FAYE AND DOLORES

FAYE

AND

DOLORES

BY BARBARA SAMUELS

BRADBURY PRESS
New York

Bradbury Press
An Affiliate of Macmillan, Inc.
866 Third Avenue, New York, N.Y. 10022
Collier Macmillan Canada, Inc.
Manufactured in the United States of America
The text of this book is set in 14 pt. Bembo Medium.
The illustrations are pen drawings with watercolor
and ink, reproduced in full color.
10 9 8 7 6 5 4 3 2 1
Library of Congress Cataloging in Publication Data:
Samuels, Barbara
Faye and Dolores.
Summary: Two young sisters agree and
disagree, yet remain affectionate.
[1. Sisters — Fiction] I. Title
PZ7.S1925Fay   1985   [E]   84-1612
ISBN 0-02-778120-8

To
SUSIE and FREYA,
and to
JONATHAN

PLAYTIME

One morning Dolores put on her favorite outfit.
"Play with me, Faye," she said.
"Not now, Dolores, I'm reading."

"I'll read too then," said Dolores. "I have one, two, three, four, five books and I am going to read every one."

Faye closed her book. "I've just changed my mind. I'd rather color today."

Faye took out a brand new box of crayons.

"This is a very funny book," said Dolores. "I'm so glad
I decided to read. When did you buy those crayons?"
"Yesterday," said Faye.

"Hee, hee, hee, this is the funniest book I have ever read,
but I don't feel like reading anymore. I think I'd rather
color today." Dolores took out her own set of crayons.

"I think I'll draw a flower," said Dolores.

"I'm drawing a flower," said Faye. "Draw something else."

"Faye, can I borrow your red crayon? I can't find mine."

"No, you'll break it," said Faye.

"Please, Faye, I'll be careful, I promise."

"Oh, all right," said Faye.

"I knew you'd break it!" shouted Faye.

"I didn't mean to," said Dolores. "It was an accident."

"You're so dumb, Dolores. You don't know how to read, you don't know how to color, and that is the ugliest flower I have ever seen."

Dolores hid behind a big book. No one spoke for a long, long time.
Finally Faye said, "It's very quiet in here."
Dolores blew her nose.

"It's so quiet it feels like a library," said Faye.
    Dolores turned the page and sniffed.
"Why don't we pretend it's a library," said Faye.

"I don't know how to read," said Dolores.
"You can be the librarian and check out books," said Faye.

"Can I tell you to sit still and stay in your chair?" asked Dolores.
"I guess so," said Faye.

"Will you raise your hand like this if you have a question?" asked Dolores.

"Sure," said Faye.

"Will you obey me at all times and do whatever I say?" asked Dolores.

"Okay," said Faye.

Dolores smiled, "Well then . . . "

SNACKTIME

"It's raining again," said Faye. "I hate rain."

"I'm going to make some peanut butter sandwiches,"
said Dolores.

"I'm sick of peanut butter sandwiches. It always rains when I want to play outside," grumbled Faye.

"All right," said Dolores. "Then I'll make a special sandwich from a secret recipe I made up myself."

"I don't want a sandwich, Dolores, I want to ride my bicycle."
"This isn't an ordinary sandwich," said Dolores.

"Add one sardine to some spaghetti and mix in a raw egg yolk . . ."
"Ugh!" said Faye.

"Then take three pieces of asparagus, cover them with mustard . . ."

"Are you really going to eat that thing?"

"I'm not finished yet," said Dolores. "I have to put in the grapes.

But first I have to squish them like this . . ."
"Ooh!" giggled Faye.
"And then I have to add a dried prune."
"What a mess," said Faye.

"Now all we need is some pickle juice . . ."
"Oh brother," said Faye.
"And an animal cracker for decoration–
the elephants have the most flavor . . ."

"Now it's all ready to eat. Doesn't it look delicious?" said Dolores.
"That is the most disgusting sandwich I've ever seen," said Faye.
"You're not really going to eat that thing, are you, Dolores?"

"Don't be silly," said Dolores. "I made it all for you, Faye.
I'm going to have a peanut butter sandwich."

BEDTIME

Dolores and Faye were getting ready for bed.
"I remember when I was so little I couldn't reach
the sink," said Dolores.

"You weren't too little to reach the toothpaste," said Faye.
"I remember the time you ate nearly half a tube."

Dolores laughed. "I was funny then. I used to chew on soapy washcloths."

"Mommy and I had to hide the soap and the toothpaste," said Faye.

"I still chew on washcloths but never when they have soap in them," said Dolores.

"Do you remember the dance I used to do when I didn't want to go to bed? I think it went like this:

"I used to think it was a lot of fun."

"Remember when you thought there was a crocodile living in the toilet?" asked Faye.

"I wouldn't walk into the bathroom until you flushed the toilet three times," said Dolores.

"Then you thought there was a snake in the hamper," said Faye.
"You would cry every time I threw my clothes in."
"I was a baby then," said Dolores. "I was scared of everything."

Dolores and Faye went into their bedroom and turned off the lights.

It was very quiet.

"Faye, I just remembered another thing I used to think when I was little.

I used to think there was something furry with bulgy eyes sitting on the dresser staring at me."

"And nothing was ever there," yawned Faye. "Good-night, Dolores."
"But I used to think there was," said Dolores.

"Do you remember what I used to ask you to do, Faye?"

"Go to sleep, Dolores."

"I think I used to ask you to get up and check the dresser just to make sure."

Faye put her head under the pillow.

"When I asked you to check the dresser what did you do, Faye?"

"I'm too tired to get up, Dolores."

"PLEASE SHOW ME, FAYE! I FORGOT HOW YOU USED TO DO IT!"

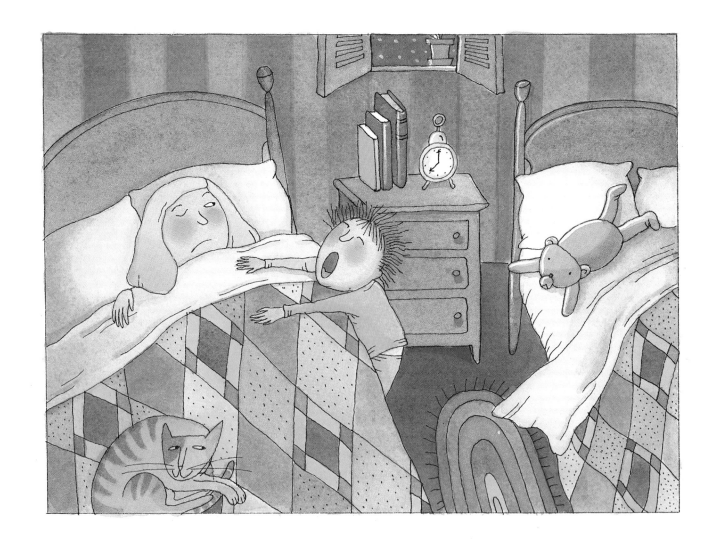

"Oh, all right," said Faye, and she got out of bed and turned on the lights. "See Dolores, it's just the red sweater you wore yesterday."

"That's what you used to do," said Dolores, "now I remember.
And then I would say, 'Good-night, Faye.'"
"Good-night, Dolores."